Please Don't Step On the Ants

Written and Illustrated by Ross Anthony

To Lionel *(the original Mr. Samblee)*

and Harry Manaka, Sr. *(in memory of)*

www.RossAnthony.com/books
For other Books, Essays & Articles by Ross Anthony

ISBN 0-9727894-4-8   ISBN13: 978-0-9727894-4-8
First print run 1/2006   10 9 8 7 6 5 4 3 2 1

Mom wakes me up early.
She reminds me to bring
an apple for my teacher. But I forget.

媽媽早早地叫我起床。她讓我別忘了給老師帶個**蘋果**。
妈妈早早地叫我起床。她让我别忘了给老师带个**苹果**。
Mi mamá me despierta muy temprano. Me recuerda de llevarle una **manzana** a mi maestro. Pero se me olvida.
私は朝早くママにおこされてしまった。ママが先生のためにリンゴを持っていきなさいと言っていたのにもかかわらず私は忘れてしまった。
Mama ananiamsha mapema. anikumbushe kupelekea mwalimu **tunda** na nikasahau
نسيت. ماما تيقظني باكراً ، وهي تذكرني بإحضار **تفاحة** إلي مُدرستي، لكنني
ตอน แม่ ของ ฉัน ปลุก ฉัน เช้า พอได้เตือนให้ฉัน เอา **แอปเปิ้ล** ไป ให้ คุณครู ของฉันด้วย แต่ปรากฏว่า ฉันลืมเอาไป
Maman me réveille tôt. Elle me rappelle d'emmener une **pomme** pour le maître. Mais j'oublie.

Mr. Samblee stands at the end of his picket fence.

桑伯利先生站在他家的白**柵欄**的頭上。
桑伯利先生站在他家的白**栅栏**的头上。
El Sr. Samblee está parado a la orilla de su **barda** de madera blanca.
サンブリーおじさんが白い**かきね**のへいの はじに立っている。
Bwana Samblee anasimama mwisho wa **ukuta** mweupe
. الأبيض ١ **الخشبي** بيته في يقف سامبلي السيّد
ﻤﺮ. แซมบลี ยืนอยู่ที่ ปลาย สุด ของ รั้ว ไม้สีขาวของเค้า
M. Samblee se tient au bout de sa **clôture** de bois blanc.

Zany the cat sneaks through the fence to play with the squirrel that lives in the yard.

那隻叫扎妮的**貓**偷偷地鑽進柵欄來跟住在
院子裡的小鬆鼠玩。
那只叫扎妮的**猫**偷偷地鉆进栅栏来跟住在
院子里的小松鼠玩。

El **gato**, Zany, se mete entre la barda para jugar con la ardilla que vive en el jardín

猫のゼイニーは オンブリーおじさんのお庭に住んでいるリスと あそぶ ために いっそりかきねの中に入る

PAKA Ziny apitia ukutani akacheze na mweu ana-yeichi kwenye uwanja

رأى **القط** يتسلل عبر الحاجز ليلعب مع السنجاب الذي يعيش في
الحوش

แมวแซน แอบ ลอด รั้ว ไป เล่น กับ กระรอก ที่ อาศัย อยู่ ในสนามหญ้า

Zany le **chat** se faufile entre les piquets de la clôture pour jouer avec
l'écureil qui vit dans le jardin.

Steam rises from Mr. Samblee's coffee like fireflies.
Puffs float off like ants caught in the wind.

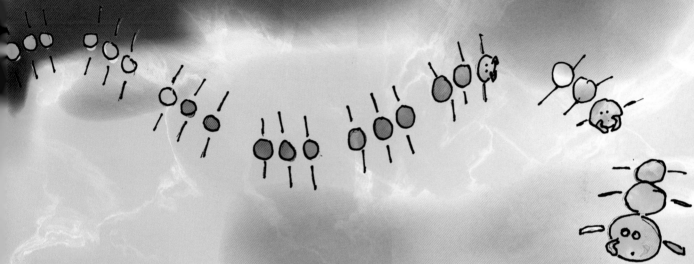

桑伯利先生的咖啡盃子裡升起來的熱氣好像
飛來飛去的螢火蟲, 冒出的泡泡像隨風漂浮的螞蟻.
桑伯利先生的咖啡杯子里升起来的热气好像
飞来飞去的萤火虫, 冒出的泡泡像随风漂浮的蚂蚁.

El vapor de la taza de café del Sr. Samblee sube como luciérnagas.
El vapor flota como si fuera hormiguitas sopladas por el viento.

サンブリーおじいさんのコーヒーから でる やけが する てほたるのように.
やが けむりは あたかも アリが 風の中に まきこまれるように ふらふでいく.

Mfuko unatokea Kwenye Kahawa ya Bwi. Samblee i. Kama wadudu Hewani

ينحصر في القهوة التي يرتقع من قهوة مستر سامبلي مثل الراعه. ينفخ العفة مثل النمل

[Lao script text]

La vapeur s'élève du café de M. Samblee, pareille à des lucioles.
Des bouffées de vapeur flottent dans l'air comme fourmis attrapées
par le vent.

Mr. Samblee really likes his coffee.
He likes the ants even more.

桑伯利先生真的喜歡他的咖啡。他更喜歡螞蟻。

桑伯利先生真的喜欢他的咖啡，他更喜欢蚂蚁。

Al Sr. Samblee le gusta mucho su **café**.
Pero las hormigas le gustan todavía más.

サンブリーおじさんはコーヒーがお気に入り。でもアリのほうがもっとお気に入り。

Bwana samblee apenda **Kahawa** yake lakini zaidi apenda wadudu

مستر سامبلي يحب حقًا قهوته (و هو يحب النمل أكثر

มส. แซมบลี ชอบ **กาแฟ** ของเขามาก แต่ชอบ มด มากกว่ามากๆ

M. Samblee aime vraiment son **café**
Mais il aime les fourmis encore plus.

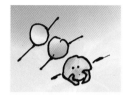

We pass Mr. Samblee's ants every morning.

我們每天早上都路過桑伯利先生的螞蟻。
我們每天早上都路过桑伯利先生的蚂蚁。
Todas las mañanas pasamos cerca de donde
están las hormigas del Sr. Samblee.
私たちは、毎朝サンブリーおじさんのアリたちをみかけて通りすぎる。
Twabita wachudu wa Bwana Samblee kila asubuhi
نحن نمر على نمل السيد سامبلي كل صباح .
พวกเราเดิน ผ่าน มด ของ มร. แซมบลีทุก ๆ เช้า
Nous passons à côté des fourmis
de M. Samblee tous les matins.

"Please don't step on the ants!"
Mr. Samblee warns.

別踩著螞蟻！" 桑伯利先生警告我們。
"別踩著螞蚁！" 桑伯利先生警告我们。

"¡No pisen las hormigas!" nos avisa el Sr. Samblee.

サンブリーおじさんが"アリたちを ふむな"と注意する

usikanyange wadudu Bwana Samblee aonya

. الأرض على تمشي لا بأن جاره يطلب سمبلي السيد

"อย่าเดินเหยียบมดนะ" มร. แซมบลี เตือนหากเรา

"Ne marchez pas sur les fourmis!"
nous avertit M. Samblee.

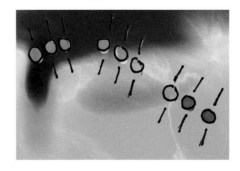

My sister hops over the ants on her pogo stick.

我妹妹站在她的蹦蹦棍上跳過螞蟻。
我妹妹站在她的蹦蹦棍上跳过蚂蚁.
Mi **hermana** brinca sobre las hormigas con su palo saltador.
妹がたけうまでアリたちを とびこえる.
Dada jangu anaruka waduchu akikanyanga mt
أختي تقفز من على النمل بعصي القفازة.
น้องสาวฉัน กระโดดข้ามเท้ามดจากมด ด้วย โพโก้ สตึ๊กต์
Ma **soeur** saute par-dessus
les fourmis avec son échasse à ressort.

Ricky takes a few steps, then dives into a somersault. I love to watch him roll.

端琦跑上幾步就地滾過去。我可**愛**看他打滾了。

端琦跑上几步就地滚过去。我可**愛**看他打滚了。

Ricky da unos pasos y luego se hecha una maroma. Me **encanta** su maroma.

リッキーが2、3歩 あるいてから でんぐりがえしをする。私はそれを見るのが**好た**。

Ricky analuka juu alafu anafanya mpingo. **Napenda** kumuona hivi

گو یہ آغاز عدہ غظوات وبعدھا بلعب المَعب **أحب** أں اراه يتحرك

ริกกี้ เดินไป สองสามก้าว แล้วก็ตีลังกา ฉันชอบดูเก้าก้า อย่างนั้นจัง

Ricky prend quelques pas puis fait un culbute. J'**adore** le voir tourner sur lui-même.

Ricky's big brother, John,
makes a huge cartwheel over the ants.

端琦的哥哥約翰翻一個車輪式的大跟頭越過螞蟻。

端琦的哥哥约翰翻一个车轮式的大跟头越过蚂蚁。

Juan, el hermano mayor de Ricky, hace una **marometa** sobre las hormigas.

リッキーのお兄さんの ジョンが アリの上を ばとんてんする。

John ndugu mkubwa wa Ricky anruka juu ya wadudu kwa **mfiringo**

اخ ريكي الكبير لركي ، جون يعمل **لفة** كبيره فوق النمل

พี่ชาย ของ ริกกี้. จอห์น, ตีลังกาท่าเท้าพากหมด

Le grand frère de Ricky, Jean, fait une grande roue
par dessus les fourmis.

I tiptoe around the ants.

我踮著腳尖繞過螞蟻。其實，螞蟻也跟我們差不多。

我踮着脚尖绕过蚂蚁。其实 蚂蚁也跟 我们差不多。

Yo camino de puntillas para no pisar las hormigas.
En muchas maneras, las hormigas son igual que nosotros.

私は 爪先で アリのまわりを しのび足で あるく、アリは なんだか私たちみたいだ。

Pole pole nasimama wacudu, wao ni kama sisi hivi

شيْت بقدم حول النمل و بنتشي ما عم

 נוּיִבְּן קפֿעָ̀ם m̀ רו רוו ו_χrora ו_χroiרן ū̀oñ i_χroru y וֹ

Je passe à côté des fourmis sur la pointe des pieds.
Elles nous ressemblent en quelque sorte.

In some ways they're just like us.

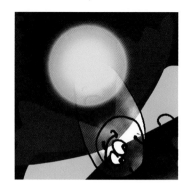

My mom says kids have a warm glow like fireflies.
So I don't step on fireflies either.

我媽媽說小孩子也跟螢火蟲一樣發著
溫暖的光。所以我也不踩螢火蟲。

我妈妈说小孩子也跟萤火虫一样发着温暖
的光，所以我也不踩萤火虫。

Mi mamá dice que a veces los niños brillan como luciérnagas.
Por eso trato de no pisar las luciérnagas.

僕は ほたるのように あたたかい光をもっていると ママが言っている。
だから 私は ほたるも ふんだりしない。

Mama anasema watoto ni kama nzi wekundu.
Kwa hivyo siwakanyangi

أمي تقول أن الأولاد يضيئون شيءً ما
اليراعين. لذلك لا أدوس على اليراعين.

คุณแม่ บอกว่า บางทีเด็กก็ส่องแสง สีไฟ อุ่น เหมือนหิ่งห้อย
ดังนั้น ฉัน ก็ไม่ เหยียบ ตัว หิ่งห้อย เหมือนกัน

Ma mère me dit que les enfants émettent une lueur chaude comme
les lucioles. Ainsi je ne marche pas non plus sur les lucioles.

I sure hope there's some huge giant like Mr. Samblee standing at the edge of some huge fence watching us walk to school.

我非常希望有桑伯利先生那樣的巨人站在
什麼巨大栅欄的頭上有著我們走路去上學
我非常希望有桑伯利先先那种的巨人站在
什么巨大栅栏的头上看着我们走路去上学。

Me gustaría confiar que hay un gigante parecido al Sr. Samblee
parado a la orilla de una barda grandísima, cuidándonos
mientras que caminamos a la escuela.

私たちが学校へと あるいているところを サンブリーおじさんのように 大きな巨人が かきねの はじに立って
みまもって くれているといいな。

14. Ningetamani Kuna jitu Kubwa Kama Samblee
Lachunga watoto waendapo Shule

أتمنى حقاً أن هناك شيء ضخم مثل مستر سايبلى بجانب الحاجز الضخم
يرافقنا في طريقنا إلى المدرسة.

J'espère bien qu'il y a un immense géant pareil à M. Samblee
debout au bout d'une immense clôture qui nous surveille quand
nous marchons à l'école.

Maybe he's so big that we can't see him,
just like the ants can't see us.

I sure hope
he's warning the other giants.
"Please don't step on the humans!"

☎ PHONE

800-ROSS-186 (1-800-767-7186)
*Schedule Ross to **SPEAK • PRESENT • INSPIRE***

✉ MAIL ORDERS

Ross Anthony, P.O. Box 5 Pasadena, CA 91102
Cal Tax included in price—Shipping/Handling...$5
Pay to the Order of Ross Anthony * Include your ship-to address
These prices good through 2006 after that—inquire by phone.
Author Signed copies available—add 2 dollars per book.
Ants...$10   Snail...$10   Rodney...$10   Jinshirou...$10   Eddie...$10

💻 ONLINE

Read excerpts from other Ross Anthony books: www.RossAnthony.com/books
www.HollywoodReportCard.com Film Reviews and Interviews by Ross Anthony

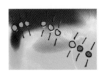

Activities and Questions

1. Some ants have wings. Which ones? And why?
2. Once an ant discovers food, how does it let other ants know how to find it?
3. Mr. Samblee protects the ants. Do ants protect another kind of creature?
4. Ask your teacher or your parents to help you make a living ant habitat.
5. Are ants cleaner than humans?
6. What are some ways to help ants stay outside your house without stepping on them?
7. You're an ant in Mr. Samblee's backyard. What is your average day like? What do you see? Taste? Smell? Hear?
8. Did you know ants have two stomachs? Find out why.
9. Find Mexico, China, Japan, Palestine, Kenya, France, Thailand and the USA on a map of the world or a globe.
10. Is China the only country where people speak Chinese? Why are there two kinds of written Chinese?
11. Besides Mexico and Spain, in what other countries is Spanish the main language?
12. Write to Ross Anthony and tell him your favorite parts of the book: Ross@rossanthony.com. (Subject line "ANTS" in capital letters.)